THIS
BOOK
BELONGS
TO

Rebecca
Plack

CAMELOT MARIAN T. PLACE was born in Gary, Indiana, raised in Minneapolis, and attended the University of Minnesota and Rollins College. Formerly a children's librarian, she has written over 200 feature articles as well as twenty-five other books for children, among them THE WITCH WHO SAVED HALLOWEEN. Mrs. Place and her husband now live in Portland, Oregon.

The Resident Witch

Marian T. Place

Illustrated by Marilyn Miller

 CAMELOT BOOKS/PUBLISHED BY AVON

AVON BOOKS
A division of
The Hearst Corporation
959 Eighth Avenue
New York, New York 10019

First Camelot Printing, October, 1973.

Third Printing

CAMELOT TRADEMARK REG. U.S. PAT. OFF.
AND IN OTHER COUNTRIES,
MARCA REGISTRADA, HECHO EN U.S.A.

Printed in the U.S.A.

TO
KRISTA

THE
RESIDENT
WITCH

ONE HOUR after the sun set two witches, one old and the other young, began to stir inside a deserted barn on the edge of a big city. At first the old witch flitted about lopsidedly because she was not yet wide awake. The young one, in her four-poster bed under the eaves, poked one foot out from under her warm covers. Brrr! Even if it was springtime, her room was cold. She burrowed under the quilts again.

Soon the old witch called out in a ratchety voice, "Witcheena, time to get up! It's broad dark outside."

The young witch buried her head under her pillow. She did not answer.

The old witch called louder. "You will be late on your scare route if you sleep all night." When Witcheena still did not answer, the old witch said, "If you do not get up this very minute and do your practicing, you will never fly up to junior witching."

The witchling groaned. It was no use. She had to get up. "Coming, Auntie," she answered sleepily. Moments later she hopped out of bed. Quickly she pulled off her pajamas and dropped them on the floor. She put on her polka-dotted underwear, long striped stockings, and a ragged brown skirt and blouse. Her slippers were brown, with big buckles and pointed toes. She plopped a pointed hat on her head and still yawning, clambered down a ladder into the kitchen. Because her bones were not yet dried out, she did not rattle the way her aunt did. But Witcheena did not worry about it. That was one of the groans of growing up. In time she would rattle as loudly as any grown-up witch.

"Evening, Auntie," she greeted the old witch. Witcheena lived with her aunt while her mother was away. Her mother belonged to a new group of witches called *Pioneers*. It was their job to explore the planets before earthlings got there. Witches couldn't stand having earthlings know more about a place than they did. Besides, they didn't want earthlings to find a place where they could hide from witches.

"Evening, dearie," her aunt answered. She peered

at her niece from under her bushy black eyebrows. "You didn't wash your face, did you?"

Witcheena shook her head. "Oh, no. I don't want a pretty face. I want to be dark and wrinkled like you."

Auntie nodded. "Good girl." She smiled fondly at her niece. "Your hair looks just like a rat's nest. But give your skirt a twitch. It's too straight."

Witcheena pulled the skirt so it sagged in back. She was glad the hem was uneven. She hoped she was getting to look more like a grown-up witch every day.

"May I help with breakfast?" she offered politely.

"No, thanks, dearie." Actually Auntie did not fuss much with cooking. She pointed her finger at the fireplace, and a fire started burning. She put on the kettle. It never was empty. Every dawn when she returned from her haunting trips around the county, she brought back things for the stew. Tonight she was serving her Special Spiced Gluck. It was made with frogs, skunk cabbage and snails. "You may bring in the evening paper, if you like."

"All right."

Witcheena left the kitchen, now bright and warm with firelight. She tried to skip, but tripped on the pointed toes. "Oh, bats!" she cried, disgusted with her clumsiness. She wished young witches, about to fly up to junior witching, did not have to wear shoes with pointed toes. Her old tennis shoes had been so much more comfortable. But she had pestered and pestered for the pointed toes. Now that she had them, she really did not like them.

When she said, "Oh, bats!" the bats clinging to the ceiling took flight. They swarmed out a hole in the roof. Their squeaking sounded like a hundred pieces of chalk scraping on a blackboard.

"Sorry I disturbed you," Witcheena apologized to them. Bats were nice pets, but terribly sensitive.

A yellow cat loomed out of the darkness, and purred about Witcheena's ankles. "Angela!" She scratched the cat's ears. "How are you tonight?"

Angela meowed so it sounded like, "Fine, thank you." Being a witchling, Witcheena understood such cat talk.

When Witcheena looked up to the barn rafters, she could see her other pet cats. All twenty-five of them. "Hello, darlings," she called.

"Meow-r-r-r," they chorused politely. Most were washing their faces and paws, or twitching their tails. Soon they would slip out, either to battle strange city cats, or to join them in a songfest, depending on whether or not there was a moon. Their eyes flickered in the dark like fireflies. This helped Witcheena find her way to the door.

Witcheena did not bother opening the barn door. It was too big for her to push, and the hinges were rusty. Besides, she needed practice going through heavy timbers. So she kicked the door, said a magic word, and passed on through to the outside. Her skirt caught on a splinter, and tore. She didn't care. There at her feet lay the evening newspaper. A copy always blew off the delivery truck when it passed on the freeway nearby. Her aunt, being a Senior Witch, was able to re-arrange the air currents so the paper landed right at the door.

Now that she was outside, Witcheena took a deep breath. She filled her lungs with the night air. A friendly fog had crept in on wet feet, and cast its clammy cloak over the trees and rocks behind the barn. It swirled along a dirty creek choked with worn-out tires and crumpled car fenders. Long ago the barn and creek had been part of a pleasant farm. Now it was a graveyard for wrecked automobiles and junked cars.

Witcheena sighed happily. She loved her home, even though she had not lived there long. She and Auntie had been driven from their former haunt, a deserted mansion. It had been bulldozed away, and replaced with a shiny glass-walled factory. For a while the two witches had despaired of finding a place suitable for them and all their bats and cats. They could not move into the adjoining county because the Supreme Witch, president of the Organization of American Witches, had assigned them this one along the coast. Every county in the United States had one or more witches assigned to it, depending on its size. All witches signed an agreement not to trespass on one another's territory. So Witcheena and her aunt had to stay where they were.

Fortunately one night while flying around the edge of the big city on her broomstick, Auntie had spotted the old barn in the middle of the junkyard. "Isn't it perfect?" she exclaimed, when she brought Witcheena to see it.

"Oh, yes," Witcheena had said, her green eyes glowing happily. The barn was the only dark quiet deserted building within miles. There was a hole in the roof for the bats to come and go freely, and rafter space for all the cats.

Around the barn were hundreds of dilapidated car bodies. The trunks were handy for Witcheena to practice skinning through locks, and hiding. The battered skeletons of once-gleaming sedans and station wagons, some piled one atop the other, made splendid hurdles for her to practice broom take-offs and landings. There were hubcaps galore, to turn into turtles; wire springs to conjure into wriggly snakes; dashboard buttons easily changed into frogs. There were no street lights, no traffic, and no night time visitors, except strange cats. Inside the junkyard, which was closed in by a high fence, it was eerily quiet save for the distant swish-swish-swish sounds made by cars whizzing past on the freeway.

Just then Auntie called from inside, "Breakfast is ready, dearie."

"Com-ing!" Witcheena sang out.

She picked up the newspaper and slipped through the door. This time she did not tear her skirt. Good! Her witching power must be growing stronger, after all. It was about time! She had been a witchling for ages and ages. She couldn't wait to try a difficult test so she could fly up to the important rank of Junior Witch.

2

As WITCHEENA stepped back into the kitchen, she smiled at her elderly aunt. Auntie was so kind. She insisted Witcheena have a nice home, so she had turned one corner of the barn into a cozy apartment. She had turned old barrels into a large and a small rocking chair, a big crate into a kitchen cabinet, and another into a table, and feed sacks into curtains and quilts. Auntie boasted to her sister witches, who came for hot brew every fourth Thursday before their evening flight, that she set the prettiest table in witchdom. Her dishes were made of sparkling glass from old car headlights.

Witcheena slipped into a chair at the table. She spread a cobweb napkin over her lap. Now that she was growing up, which took ages in witchdom, she did not have to tuck the napkin under her chin any

8

more. She sniffed happily. "Mmmm, the stew smells yummy. I'm hungry."

Auntie took a taste. "Yes, it is good. You may have a second helping, if you wish. Oh, tut-tut-tut! Eat slowly. Mind your table manners. Eat like a little lady."

"Yes, ma'am." Witcheena took small bites. She chewed quietly with her mouth closed. After she finished eating, she stamped her foot, said a magic word, pointed her finger at the dishes. They washed themselves clean and put themselves in the cabinet. "Shall I sweep the floor?" she asked.

Auntie though a moment. "No, this is the day the mice come in. They will clean up the crumbs." She had moved to her cooking chair by the fireplace. "You do your practicing now. I want to read the newspaper."

Witcheena made a face and said in a whining voice, "Do I have to?"

"Certainly. How else will you pass the tests so you can fly up to junior witching?"

"Oh, bats," Witcheena groaned. However, since she was an obedient little witchling, she practiced. For five minutes she pulled and pinched her nose so it would grow long and pointed. Then she cracked her knuckles twenty times. She also did her squawking and cackling scales. Finally she recited softly the magic phrases which all witches must learn. There were a great many.

For instance, if she wanted to make it rain, she could not just point her finger and say, "Rain." Or, "Rain, *please*." She had to say, *"Ab-dib-wurp,* rain!" Without the correct magic phrase, nothing would happen. If she got mixed up, or forgot and said the wrong phrase, such as *"ab-dab-ghee,"* before the word "rain", it would not rain. Since there was a different phrase for each prank or task, memorizing the long list was very, very hard.

When Witcheena finished practicing, she flopped down in her rocking chair to rest. After a bit she asked, "Auntie, haven't you finished reading the paper yet?" She never did like to sit still long, especially when it was broad dark outside.

"Not quite," Auntie told her. "I have not read about one single thing we can haunt tonight."

"Then may I turn on the Space Tube set? It's time for the Walt Dizzy program."

When her aunt nodded, Witcheena pulled the *On* knob. The sound whistled and cracked. Blurry pictures from several planets rolled on the screen. After the picture cleared, Witcheena watched a film about a boy from Mars who rode a space craft to the earth in order to capture wild animals for the Mars zoo. It was terribly exciting.

During the commercial Witcheena closed her eyes and stuck her fingers in her ears. She dreamed she was riding a space craft. It looked like the one the two astronauts rode to the moon and back. She soared and zipped among the stars. She chased a comet. She tried to play tag with Telstar, one of the Earth's satellites. But Telstar ignored her, and went right on bleeping and blinking.

After she stopped dreaming, she wished for a space craft of her own. But she dared not make one with her witchcraft, even if her power was strong enough, which it wasn't. All the Senior Witches disapproved of space craft. They took a vow never to give up their brooms for moon ships. In fact, every year at their annual convention held the week after Halloween, they promised not to think up the proper magic phrase for making one. Without the proper magic phrase they couldn't conjure up a satellite or a flying saucer or a lunar module. At least, that's what Auntie had told her.

But the more Witcheena thought about a moon ship, the more she was positive that riding in one would be much easier than traveling through space on a broom. A broom was scratchy, and hard for a

11

witchling to steer. So far, every time she got caught in a down draft, she had splashed *ker-plunk* into a pool or a fountain, and once into a bird bath. Awful! The landings and take-offs were not easy, either. She was forever tumbling on her head, or slipping off the bristles. That's why she had to practice landings and take-offs so much.

She interrupted her aunt's reading. "Auntie, by the time I graduate to Senior Witch rank, will we all be riding around in moon ships?"

Her aunt snorted. "Certainly not! No witch with any respect for her magic would give up her broom."

"But riding a broom is uncomfortable, and cold sometimes. Besides, it's oldfashioned. A moon ship is the modern way to fly."

Auntie rocked noisily. "Oh, you youngsters! You are never satisfied with things as they are. You always want to change them. I don't want to hear another word about a moon ship or any other kind of space craft."

"All right," Witcheena answered in a small voice. She went back to watching her favorite program. "But some day," she promised herself, "I am going to ride in a moon ship!" That way she could go on a pioneering flight like her mother and enjoy it. Poor Mama! It must be awfully cold flying through space on a broom. And lonesome, too. In a moon ship there would be room for two companions and Angela, too.

Suddenly Auntie jabbed the newspaper with a bony finger. "Aha! Here is something you can do tonight."

Witcheena's eyes flickered excitedly. "What?"

"It says here that there is a carnival over at the

supermarket." The old witch cackled. "You broom right over there and ruin the fun!"

"But how?" Witcheena asked. Ruining a carnival was an awfully big task for a witchling.

"That's up to you," Auntie answered. Then she twitched bushy eyebrows, and said slowly, "This could be a very important test, dearie."

"Honestly?" Witcheena bounded out of her chair and danced for joy. However, because she was young and awkward, and not used to her pointed shoes, she flip-flopped. She picked herself up. "May I take Angela?"

"Don't you want to do this on your very own? If you remember all I have taught you, you shouldn't have any trouble. Just don't try to do too much. After all, your witch powers are not fully developed yet."

Witcheena knew that, so she said politely, "Yes, ma'am."

"Have a good time, and be home by midnight."

"By midnight!" Witcheena wailed. "That early?"

"Midnight is late enough for a witchling."

"Oh, all right." Witcheena kissed her aunt on the cheek, and clumped out. "Bats!" she muttered to herself. "I always have to be home early."

She slipped through the barn door and mounted

her broom. She sat on the bristles, with her legs folded under her, and grasped the handle firmly. "All right, Cadenza," she told the broom, "let's go. But easy, now. Don't jet off without me."

Cadenza rocketed into the air.

3

THE FLIGHT to the roof of the supermarket was a short one. There was no fog there. Cadenza made a butter-smooth landing. After Witcheena laid the broom aside gently, she looked over the carnival. The lights were beautiful, even if they did make her squint. There was music everywhere. She could see some boys and girls whirling around on a big wheel, and riding ponies on a merry-go-round.

Witcheena rubbed her hands and cackled, the way her aunt would have done. Oh, she was going to enjoy ruining the carnival. It was the first big task that would count toward earning her rank of Junior Witch. She must not fail.

She rubbed her nose. What should she do? Make it rain? Of course! But she would make it rain only over the carnival, so she would not get wet. She hated water in any form, and particularly rain. Whenever she was caught out in the rain, her skirt became water-logged, and her pointed hat drooped. Also, the rain washed her face. Having a clean face was one of the worst things that could happen to a witchling. It took ages to acquire a deep even dirt-tan.

So Witcheena stamped, said the magic make-it-rain words, and pointed toward the carnival. A few sprinkles fell, but not enough to send the boys and girls scurrying for cover. She was terribly disappointed. Although her witch power was growing stronger, it was not yet strong enough to brew up a cloudburst.

She rubbed her nose again, and thought hard. What to try next? Suddenly her green eyes glowed. If she put out all the lights, the people having fun would have to go home.

She stamped, said the magic put-out-the-lights word, and pointed one finger at the main electric switch. Blue sparks sputtered. The lights flashed off all over the supermarket and carnival. Even the music died out.

Witcheena jigged for joy on the roof top. She had done it!

However, in about thirty seconds, the electricity

17

came back on. The carnival soon was in full swing again.

"Oh, bats!" Witcheena pouted. A fine chance she had of passing her test at this rate.

She thought hard some more. Maybe she could huff and puff, and blow down all the tents and rides. She took such a deep breath and sucked in her stomach so much that her skirt nearly fell off. Then she exhaled noisily. But nothing happened. She had forgotten to stamp her foot and say the magic blow-wind-blow words. Now she would have to rest because she had used up so much of her witching power. She would have to wait until it built up again. That was one of the groans of being a witchling. Her power was not steady, as it would be much later on when she became a Senior Witch.

Witcheena sat down with her pointed shoes dangling over the edge of the roof. She studied the carnival because she had never seen one this close before. My, there were so many things going on at the same time, things she could upset with Junior Witch pranks. She could hardly wait for her power to recharge. Maybe she could make the Ferris wheel spin backwards? Suppose she made the ponies on the merry-go-round squeal? Or switch their tails? That would scare the riders. Whee! She rubbed her hands, and cackled again.

Her eyes narrowed to slits as she peered at the boys and girls. She always wondered what young

earthlings did for fun. She knew they rode bicycles and skates instead of brooms, and liked water sports. They also ate strange food with lots of finger-licking, which Auntie considered very bad manners. And when they laughed, they did not cackle. They laughed most when they played on school grounds.

However, Auntie assured her, they groaned awfully in their classrooms. But except for school, they had fun. And they shared their fun with friends.

Sharing with friends her age was something she had never enjoyed. She had no friends. Remembering this made her so sad that she almost cried. Of course, she could not really cry because witches cannot shed tears. They cry dry.

True, she thought, she had Angela. The cat was a wonderful companion, but she was only a cat, not a girl witchling. Witcheena wished she had someone her own age to talk to, and fly around with, and share secrets and cackles. The only time she got to play with other witchlings was at the national witches' convention held every year near Chicago. She and Auntie would fly there in the fall, after Hallowe'en, so she could advance to her Junior Witch rank. But meantime she had no dear friends because there were no other witchlings west of the Rocky Mountains. There were several in New England, and three in the South, but she was the only one in the West. Witchlings were *very* rare. That made her special. Still she would rather be less special and have a friend.

Witcheena sighed. She would love to flit down onto the carnival grounds and have fun with a friend.

It wasn't fair having to perch on a roof top all by herself. The longer she watched the happy earthlings, the more she hated being alone. She became so lonesome that her heart ached fiercely. Oh, dear, wasn't there something she could do?

She pressed the end of her nose with her little finger, and thought and thought. After a bit she had a marvelous idea. It made the peak of her hat twitch, and her shoe buckles quiver. Why not join the carnival crowd? For a moment she rocked with joy. But then she shivered. Did she dare? Her aunt would be very angry if she found out. Still it would be fun to do something naughty. The chance of getting caught was very small. Auntie was off somewhere, busy with her senior witching.

Witcheena took a deep breath. She said boldly, "I'll do it!"

Quickly she climbed on her broom and jetted off the roof top.

A MOMENT later Witcheena and Cadenza touched down on the shadowy edge of the carnival grounds. After leaning the broom against a telephone pole, she looked about timidly. This was her first time being near earthlings who could see her. But the boys and girls looked so happy and friendly that she forgot to be nervous, and stepped out into the open. Then she stopped so suddenly that she almost tripped. Her clothes! She could not mingle with earthlings wearing her brown witchling's uniform. She could not make herself invisible yet because only Senior Witches had power enough to do that.

Once more Witcheena pressed the tip of her nose until another idea popped into her head. Of course! She would change into an earth girl. But her eyes widened. "I wonder if I have enough power left to do that." She had never tried such a difficult task.

What if she failed? And what should she wear? She must think carefully, and have her costume in mind before she made the change.

First, though, she hopped back behind the telephone pole. Then she peered around it in order to study the girl earthlings. The lights bothered her eyes so that she could hardly see. But finally she decided she should appear in shorts and a sleeveless top, and sunglasses so the glaring lights wouldn't hurt her eyes. She hugged herself tightly so she wouldn't fly to pieces, stamped her foot, and said the magic turn-into-an-earthling phrase. Her skin tingled. Her knees knocked rat-a-tat. Bells tinkled inside her head. When her brain stopped reeling and she looked at herself, she squeaked with horror. She was wearing shorts and a sleeveless top and large round sunglasses, but her long stockings and garters showed! Although she tugged and tugged, she could not pull the shorts down over her knees.

When Cadenza made a jolly rapping sound against the telephone pole, Witcheena said crossly, "You stop laughing at me, Cadenza!"

Suddenly she sneezed. She wasn't used to wearing a sleeveless top. Quickly she studied the earth girls again. This time she pictured herself in a pair of long orange stretch pants, topped with a sloppy

23

sweater of the same color, and orange-and-white stripped tennis shoes. When she repeated the magic routine, the new outfit replaced the first one. Ah, this was better! The pants covered her wrinkled stockings. Best of all, she could wiggle her toes inside the tennis shoes. Her costume was so perfect that she was sure no one would suspect she was a witch. However, she had forgotten to picture a different hair style, and her hair was still very messy.

As soon as her stomach flutters quieted, she looked about for something to do. But even though she was dressed like an earthling, she thought like a witchling. Naturally she began planning right away what pranks she might try.

As she approached the rides and booths, her eyes glittered. She was so happy that she skipped. It was nice to skip without tripping! Soon she stopped in front of a booth where a fat man was selling large inflated balloons. After making sure that no one in the noisy throng was watching, she stamped her foot, whispered the magic words, and pointed at the balloons. The air whistled out of every one, and they collapsed. The man looked so perplexed that Witcheena burst out laughing.

Next she watched a lady in a white uniform cooking French fried potatoes. When she tossed them lightly in a metal basket to drain off the grease, Witcheena made them scatter all over the top of the stove. The cook got so mad that her face turned fiery red. Witcheena chortled, and moved on. This was such fun!

Soon she came alongside the merry-go-round. She hemmed and hawed. Should she make the ponies squeal? It was so noisy though that she doubted if even the riders could hear them do it. She watched closely. When the man in charge wanted the merry-go-round to stop so the children could get off, he pulled a long metal brake handle. Witcheena bought a ticket, and climbed on a pony. When enough children clambered aboard, the man started the merry-go-round. The ponies bobbed up and down, faster and faster. The music blared. The platform spun dizzily.

Witcheena loved the ride. It was almost as much fun as riding her broom. She waved at the people, and giggled. What would they say if they knew a witch was waving at them? When the ride was supposed to end, Witcheena flummoxed the brake so it would not work. The merry-go-round spun and spun. The man grew angrier and angrier. Finally Witcheena relented, and unflummoxed the handle. The ride came to an end.

As Witcheena skipped on toward the Ferris wheel, she felt terribly bold. She wondered if she dared make friends with any of the earthlings? Not only would that be daring. According to the Witches' Rules of Behavior, it was absolutely forbidden!

Eyes shining with mischief, she skipped along. Soon she found herself facing two boys. She stopped and stared at them. Her heart went pit-a-pat. She had never looked straight into the eyes of an earthling before. The longer she looked at the boys, the more she realized they were very nice looking.

Suddenly she blurted, "Hi!" and smiled broadly at them.

The boys stared at her. Then they looked at each other, and crossed their eyes. "Boy, what a witch!" they exclaimed, gagging. They brushed past her as they went away.

Witcheena was so disappointed that she cried, even though no tears spilled down her cheeks.

A girl with long blonde hair, and wearing yellow stretch pants and a floppy sweater, had heard what the boys said. When she saw Witcheena's distress, she put her arm around her shoulders. "Don't mind. What do you care if those horrible boys called you a witch?"

Witcheena sniffed. "Oh, I am used to being called a witch. I didn't mind that. But I didn't want the boys to hurry away. I am new here. I was trying to make friends."

The girl smiled. "Be my friend. I am new here, too. I am from Oshkosh. My name is Nancy. What is yours?"

Witcheena thought wildly. She did not have an earth name. But she had heard names on the Walt Dizzy television program. "Oh . . . my name is . . . is Jane. I . . . uh . . . live out in the country."

"Keen," Nancy babbled. "I have never known anyone who lived in the country. I have always lived in a big city. Do you milk cows? Do you have cats? I have a Siamese cat. Her name is Chin Lieu, but I call her Chinny. Have you got a pet cat?"

Witcheena found Nancy's chatter hard to follow. But she nodded happily because it was fun talking to someone about her age. "My cat's name is Angela. She's not any one kind of cat. She has yellow eyes and yellow fur."

"I bet she's pretty." Nancy cocked her head sideways. "Say, would you like to borrow my comb?" She giggled. "You must have been riding The Hammer. Your hair looks like a rat's nest."

Witcheena's eyebrows raised. "It's supposed to look that way."

Nancy blinked. "Oh, pardon me. Is that the way the girls in the country wear their hair?"

"No, it's the way witches wear their hair," she answered truthfully.

Nancy looked shocked for a moment. Then she exclaimed, "Oh, you are marvelous! I love girls who talk kooky. Now tell me something else. Your skin is so dark. Are you an Indian?"

"No, I'm a witchling," Witcheena answered, without thinking.

"You're a WHAT?" Nancy shrieked. Then she bent over laughing.

Witcheena choked, and crossed her eyes. She had given away the secret that she really was a witch! A witch who betrayed her identity to earthlings turned into a toad. Instantly. And forever. Frightened, she looked down at her feet to see if they were changing shape. But they weren't, and she didn't have time to wonder why. She said hastily, "Maybe I better use your comb, Nancy." She was relieved to discover that when she tried to laugh off what she had said, she no longer cackled. Her witchling's cackle had changed to an earthling's giggle.

"You are so funny!" Nancy said when she stopped laughing. "Here, let me help you untangle the snarls in your hair." Obviously, she had not believed what Witcheena had said.

After Witcheena's hair was combed out, it hung

silkily to her shoulders. She didn't like it that way because it tickled the back of her neck. However, she did not complain for fear of offending her new friend. "Now can we do something together?" she asked.

"Yes, let's," Nancy agreed. "I want to ride on the Ferris wheel. But let's buy popcorn first. I'm starved." She didn't ask Witcheena what she wanted to do.

"Popcorn?" Witcheena had never tasted popcorn.

Nancy shrugged. "Or a hot dog. It doesn't matter to me. I'll treat."

Witcheena smiled. She loved hot dog meat. It was a witches' delicacy.

A few moments later Witcheena braced herself for her first taste of the kind of food earthlings eat. She nibbled daintily on the hot dog. It tasted terrible to her, but she did not say so. Instead she said politely, "Thank you for the treat, Nancy."

"You're welcome."

As the two strolled toward the Ferris wheel, Nancy chattered, "Don't you love carnivals? I do. I go to every one I can. I can hardly wait for the new amusement park to be built. That will be even more fun to visit than a carnival. But I guess you don't need amusement parks in the country, do you? You have lots of room to play, don't you?"

Witcheena nodded. "Lots and lots."

"Does your father run a farm? Do you have a horse? Is it really fun to slide down a haystack, or does it scratch?"

Because Witcheena was young, and wanted Nancy to know all about her so they could be good friends, she babbled without thinking again. "My family doesn't run a farm. My mother is a witch. She's been gone for months, riding a space vehicle which is supposed to take television pictures of the planet Mars. I'm living with my aunt until she gets back. She's a witch, too."

Nancy gulped, and her eyes widened. "Hunh?"

Witcheena choked with fright. She was scared pink-and-green. The first time she had given away the secret of being a witch nothing had happened to her either because it was an accident, or the first time for witchlings didn't count, or because Nancy didn't believe what she said. But now she had blurted her secret a second time, and she was bound to turn into a toad.

When Witcheena turned pink-and-green, Nancy thought her new friend was choking on her hot dog. She pounded her on the back between her shoulders. All this time she was laughing. "Oh, what a kooky story! You have a fabulous imagination!" She gave Witcheena a quick hug.

Witcheena finally stopped choking. She took a deep breath. Whew! She was safe. There was no harm done because Nancy thought she was telling a fib. Witches were allowed to tell fibs to earth people. So, since Nancy did not believe she was a witch, she would not turn into a toad after all.

Still, her narrow escape left her a little shaky. She must be very, very careful what else she said to her new friend.

31

Nancy was determined to find out more about Witcheena. "Tell the truth. Don't you live on a farm?"

Witcheena rolled her eyes, and drawled, "Well . . . it used to be a farm. Now it's a junk yard for wrecked cars."

Nancy wrinkled her nose, almost as if she had smelled something bad. "I wouldn't want to live in a junk yard. Then you don't have cows and horses?"

Even if it was dangerous and naughty, Witcheena wondered just how much she could tell without betraying her witchhood. "No. But I do have twenty-six cats and forty-twelve bats."

Nancy made a terrible face. "Forty-twelve bats? For pets? Ugh! I scream and cover my hair every time I see one. I think they're the ugliest things in the whole world."

Witcheena decided to change the subject before

she talked too much again. "What does your father do?"

As usual Nancy talked lickety-split. "My father builds amusement parks. He planned the one the city will start building soon. It will have all sorts of keen rides, and a playground with swings, and a swimming pool and tennis courts, and a volleyball court, and a baseball field. Oh, and a camping area for overnight outings."

"It sounds wonderful," Witcheena remarked. She was happy to hear about it because haunting an amusement park promised to be great fun. There weren't too many really exciting things for a witchling to haunt in a county which was almost entirely swallowed up by a big city. She could make all sorts of things go wrong in an amusement park.

"I hope your father starts building the park real soon," she added.

"So do I," Nancy said, "The kids in my neighborhood don't have any really nice place to play. There's not one single place for overnight camping, either. I belong to a Girl Scout troop. We hardly ever get to camp out overnight because most of the girls live in apartments. Nobody has a yard big enough to put up a tent and have a campfire. Say, are you a Girl Scout? I had my fly-up this spring."

"Fly-up?"

Nancy bobbed her head. "Yes. See, when you join Girl Scouts, first you are a Brownie scout. You wear a brown uniform and beanie cap, and have lots of fun. Then you fly up from Brownie Scouts to Junior Scout rank, and wear a green uniform. You have lots more fun. Next you advance to Cadet Rank, and after you enter high school, you become a Senior Scout."

Witcheena's mouth formed a small pink "o". So witchlings were not the only ones who had fly-ups, and wore brown uniforms, and graduated to junior and senior ranks! Why, she had something in common with Nancy after all. She opened her mouth to tell Nancy about her Junior witch test and fly-up. But she caught herself in time. Instead she asked, "Where is this amusement park going to be?"

"Somewhere on the edge of the city, near the freeway," Nancy said. But she was fidgeting. She did not like to stand still and talk. She wanted to be doing something exciting every minute. "If you have twenty-five cents, we can ride the Ferris wheel," she suggested.

Witcheena nodded even if she didn't have a cent in her pockets. But while walking toward the Ferris wheel she used her witch powers to fill her pants pocket with quarters. The two bought tickets, went through a turnstile, and climbed into a seat on the wheel. The seat tilted back and forth. Nancy squealed, so Witcheena squealed, too. She wanted to do everything just like her friend did. Soon they were swooping up, and over, and down. They clung to the safety bar with both hands and squealed a lot more. Evidently that was the way to act, thought Witcheena, because all the boys and girls did.

When the ride was over, Nancy said, "Now let's try the crack-the-whip." And after that wild ride finished, she said, "I want to ride the roll-a-hoop next." She never once asked Witcheena what she wanted to do. But Witcheena didn't care because every ride was different. Her biggest problem came from behaving properly. That grew to be more and more of a strain. She had to grit her teeth to keep from flummoxing something.

Finally she could not behave another minute. She couldn't help it. She had to make some mischief. At the roll-a-hoop ride, she and Nancy sat on a seat suspended between two huge hoops made of rubber tires. They fastened the safety bar, and by rocking back and forth started the hoops rolling. These

35

rolled slowly around a dirt track, following other hoops. The seat did not roll up and over; it remained level.

Witcheena thought this was a rather dull ride. When Nancy wasn't watching, she kicked the seat with her heel, said the magic turn-upside-down words, and pressed the seat with one hand. Immediately the seat rolled up and over. That was so much fun that Witcheena made their hoops roll faster. They spun merrily past other hoops, banged into others, and knocked them aside. The boys and girls riding in them squealed with delight. But their parents, watching on the sidelines, shouted in alarm. Two attendants ran out and tried to catch the runaway hoops. Witcheena made them spin on one tire, and escaped their clutches. But this caused Nancy to tumble to the ground. Witcheena stopped the contraption, and ran to her.

"Are you hurt?" she asked anxiously.

Nancy was not hurt. She laughed. "Let's do that again!"

But the men would not let them have another ride, so they walked off.

Witcheena said, "You treated me to a hot dog. Now let me treat you. What would you like?"

When they came alongside a booth offering a

game of skill, Nancy said, "Let's try our luck. If we can throw those plastic rings onto those sticks, we can win prizes."

Witcheena handed the man two quarters in exchange for twelve rings. She gave half to Nancy. Each won a green beanie hat which had a plastic propeller on top. Nancy plopped hers on her head. So did Witcheena. Then Nancy spun the propeller on hers, and flapped her arms, and rose on tiptoe.

"What are you trying to do?" Witcheena asked, wide-eyed.

"I'm trying to fly," Nancy explained. "I'm trying to get off the ground like a helicopter." She flapped her arms hard, and then said disgustedly, "Oh, fiddlesticks, I'm glued to the ground."

Witcheena felt sorry for Nancy. How awful not to be able to fly! She simply must help her. "No wonder! You forgot to stamp your foot, and say the magic words. You forgot to say *ab* . . ." Suddenly she clamped her hand over her mouth. Again she had almost given herself away.

"Say what magic words?" Nancy demanded.

Witcheena lowered her hand. "Oh, I couldn't tell you!"

"You can, too, tell me. I want to know, right this very minute," Nancy insisted, stamping her foot.

Witcheena pressed her lips together, and shook her head.

Nancy tossed her hair and said a little crossly, "All right, I'll make up my own words." She shouted, "*Abba-dabba-crick!*" But she remained on the ground. That made her so angry she clenched her fists, and said, "For two cents, I'd throw a tantrum, and scream!"

Witcheena was shocked at how quickly Nancy's disposition had changed. Why, in a few more seconds they might even stick out their tongues at each other, and walk away, and never see each other again. And she had thought they were the best of friends. Her chin began to tremble.

Nancy's cross look faded. "Let's not be mad at each other. I like you. I was hoping we could have lots of fun together."

Witcheena hugged her. "I like you, too. And let's have fun, starting right now."

The two walked along past several rides which did not interest them. Suddenly Nancy clapped her hands. "I know. Let's try the Moon Ship ride. My father says that after the astronauts walked on the moon, carnivals all over the country added Moon Ship rides. He says there's a big one at Disneyland.

I've never been on one. You aren't afraid to ride in it, are you?"

"No! I'm used to flying," Witcheena boasted. "I fly around on a broom all the time."

"You what?" Nancy's eyes nearly popped out of her head. Then she wrinkled her nose and said, "Oh, you, and your witch talk!"

Witcheena giggled, and ran to the ticket booth. She paid a quarter and walked toward a small model of a silver-colored space ship. It looked almost like the gumdrop-shaped command and service module which the astronauts used in orbiting the moon. There were eleven others just like it bolted to a huge wheel. The hub was taken up by a large model of the moon. Actually it housed the machinery needed to turn the wheel so the little moon ship models would go around and around in a make-believe orbit. Inside each little Moon Ship were three reclining couches, control wheels, and an instrument panel crowded with buttons and brightly-colored knobs.

An attendant was standing by the hatch of the Moon Ship. "Hop in," he said.

Nancy slipped through the hatch, and sat on the couch by the far window. Witcheena took the couch nearest the hatch. She was also by a window.

"Fasten your seat belts," the attendant instructed them.

Witcheena watched Nancy snap the buckle and then fixed the one on her couch. "Hmmm," she told

herself. "Seat belts are just what I need when I ride on Cadenza. Then I wouldn't fall off so much." She examined the belt and buckle carefully so she could conjure up a similar one later on.

"Sit tight," the attendant told them as he closed

the hatch. Then he helped other boys and girls into their moon ships.

While Nancy and Witcheena looked out their small windows, the witchling was seized with an enormous temptation to stamp her foot, say some magic words, and really lift off. Oh, how she ached to ride through the skies in a comfortable moon ship. She struggled so hard to control herself that her beanie cap fell off. It was just as well she did behave, she decided. Her witching power might not be strong enough to free the little space craft from the metal spoke to which it was bolted. And come to think of it, she didn't know the magic words to make it fly.

When all the moon ships were filled, the attendant started the gigantic wheel turning. Immediately colored lights flashed on the instrument panel, and each moon ship vibrated strongly, as if it really was lifting off from earth. Nancy and Witcheena were wide-eyed. "I think we're really going to the moon!" Nancy squealed. As the wheel turned faster and faster, the moon ships swooped up and up, and then down, and up again, and gyrated wildly. Witcheena gripped the control wheel in front of her. She pretended she was flying in space. Every time the craft

41

went up high, she looked outside to see if her aunt was flying up yonder. When she saw no sign of her, she grinned. Good! Auntie would not approve of her riding in a moon ship when she was supposed to be ruining the carnival.

"Oh, well," she excused herself, "there's a lot of time left for me to practice. Besides, my witching power needs lots of time to re-charge itself."

The ride was over all too soon, so she treated Nancy and herself to a second ride. On this one, Witcheena noticed something. Every time the moon ship rode high up, she could look down on a tent at the back of the Moon Ship ride. Behind the tent were three spare moon ships which rested on wooden crates. They were not bolted down. "Hmmmm," she murmured. She must remember that.

After she and Nancy left the ride, they strolled up and down with arms entwined. Never before had Witcheena been so happy. She was so glad she had not put out the carnival lights, because now she had a friend. And she was having the same kind of fun as earth boys and girls. For a tiny moment she wished she was an earthling. But immediately she felt ashamed. Such a wish was disloyal to her witch-hood. Still, she thought wistfully, being an earthling had some advantages. She loved her earth clothes.

They were colorful, and so comfortable. From the way some boys looked at her, they must make her look pretty, too.

"Do I have to go on being an oldfashioned witch?" she asked herself. "Couldn't I be just as good a witch without having a pointed nose, and a cackling laugh, and a ragged skirt, and shoes that pinch my toes?" She liked her beanie cap better than her pointed one. It was not as heavy as her witch's hat, and it was silly looking. That was the way she felt—silly and young and happy.

Suddenly a siren wailed.

"What is that?" Witcheena exclaimed.

Nancy groaned. "That's the curfew siren. I suppose you don't have one in the country. Curfew blows at nine o'clock. All city children are supposed to be home by then. I'll have to run to catch my bus." Nancy looked sad. "Gee, I hate to go. We've had such fun."

"Won't I ever see you again?" Witcheena asked.

Nancy put her arms around Witcheena's neck. "We just can't say goodbye. Not when we are getting to be such good friends." Then she stepped back, and clapped her hands. "I know! Let's meet here tomorrow night. The same place by the Ferris wheel. Okay?"

Witcheena nodded happily. "Okay," she answered. The word felt awkward on her lips.

Nancy gave her a quick hug, and dashed off to her bus. Soon she was out of sight.

Witcheena's smile faded. Her shoulders drooped. She felt lonelier and lonelier.

Then with a start, she remembered, "My test! My big test!"

She must return to being a witch at once!

WITCHEENA scurried back to Cadenza. She
hid behind the pole, and started to say the magic
words that would change her back into a witchling.
But she could not bear to part with her beanie hat.
"All right, I'll keep it," she decided boldly. The
moment she was dressed like a witchling, she cried,
"Ouch!" Her pointed shoes pinched her toes again.
Her brown uniform seemed so drab, but the beanie
fit nicely under her witch's hat. She climbed on the
broom and jetted back to the roof of the supermarket.

"Now for the test," she chortled, rubbing her
hands.

She went through her magic act and pointed her
finger at the main electric switch, *hard*. The lights
sputtered, and winked out. This time they remained
off.

Down below men shouted and waved flashlights. "The transformer has blown out," one man called out. "We won't have lights before tomorrow. We might as well shut down."

After the grounds were deserted, Witcheena thought up a new idea. It was daring, and deliciously naughty. Her eyes glittered with mischief. But before she acted, she called softly, "Auntie?"

Her aunt did not appear. The coast was clear. Cackling happily, she climbed on her broom. Cadenza lifted unevenly, and for a moment Witcheena teetered wildly on her broom. Then she pointed toward the Moon Ship ride, and landed behind the tent.

"Stay," she told Cadenza, and leaned the broom against the tent.

Next she walked to one of the extra space ships resting unattached on a big box. She opened the hatch. Immediately there was a rat-a-tatting noise. She jumped like a scared grasshopper. Her aunt had caught her! Then the noise sounded again. Whew! It was only Cadenza. Witcheena shook her finger at the broom. "Stop being jealous. I am only going for a teeny little ride. I am not deserting you."

Cadenza sagged against the canvas.

The little witchling opened the hatch and settled

herself on the couch. After buckling the safety belt she stamped her foot. But she couldn't finish her magic rigamarole because she didn't know the right magic words.

Slowly a bold idea occurred to her. Could she make up the words on her own? The thought alone made her hair stick straight out under her two hats. Auntie would be horrified! All the Senior Witches would frown. But she didn't care. She thought and thought. She tried one combination of words after another. Still nothing happened. Finally she put together the magic words for flying, and the moon, and an airship. When she repeated them very quickly, the lift-off button on the instrument panel flickered wildly. Other red, blue and green lights flashed, and the Moon Ship quivered violently!

Squeaking with glee, Witcheena pulled back on the control wheel, all the while repeating the magic words. The Moon Ship rose gently from the launching box straight up into the air.

"Whee!" she cackled. She pulled harder on the wheel. The craft zoomed higher. She flew slowly over the carnival grounds, and circled the supermarket. Then she hovered here and there. As she looked out through the window, she was not too surprised to see some people staring up at her. But when car spotlights flashed her way, she moved on. She flew all around the big city, and the surrounding country. The Moon Ship was warm and cozy. She much preferred riding in it to the outside of her scratchy broom. Not that she was disloyal to Cadenza. But riding a broom did have its disadvantages, especially in cold or rainy weather.

She grew bolder in handling the space ship. She zipped and zoomed, spiralled, rolled like a barrel, and jetted down in nose dives. She practiced touchdowns and lift-offs from the roof of the new Post Office building. She raced a jet airliner, and waved at the pilot. He shook his fist at her, so she turned away. Auntie had warned her to stay clear of aircraft. All over the world, witches stayed clear of airports and aircraft, so there would be no accidents.

There was only one thing wrong with her flight. She missed Nancy. But Nancy would never go on a witch trip. Witcheena sighed. She had learned tonight that half the fun of doing something was sharing it with someone.

After another circle around the city she returned to the carnival grounds and slowly, through the darkness, touched down on the box behind the tent. Then quickly she opened the hatch, hopped out, closed it and ran to Cadenza.

"Promise not to get even with me for riding the Moon Ship? No tricks?" she beseeched her broom.

Cadenza swayed a little. Witcheena hopped on the broom, clasped the handle firmly, and zipped up into the sky. Brrr! The night air was cold. Seconds later she landed beside the barn. She put the broom in a sheltered place and slipped through the door. In the bedroom she dropped her clothes on the floor, and put on her pajamas. By midnight she was fast asleep.

7

THE NEXT evening Witcheena wore the beanie to breakfast instead of her peaked hat. Her aunt snorted, "Where did you get that silly looking hat?"

"At the carnival."

Auntie stirred a pot of beet soup thickened with seaweed. "Well, if you snatched it from some earthling, it's all right."

Witcheena did not explain how she got the beanie. She ran to get the paper, and only somersaulted once. After breakfast Auntie read while Witcheena practiced. All of a sudden the old witch began to rock faster. "Ah! I see you shut down the carnival last night. Good girl! It says here that a power failure made the lights go out, so the carnival had to close." Her aunt cackled, "I'm very proud of your work, dearie. Ruining the carnival will count a lot to prove you are ready to fly up to junior witching."

Witcheena bragged, "I also made trouble for the balloon seller . . . uh . . . before I put the lights out. And I flummoxed the merry-go-round and roll-a-hoop rides." She was careful not to say anything

about enjoying herself or going around with Nancy. But she did add impatiently, "Auntie, when is my power going to be as strong and steady as yours?"

"Just be patient, dearie," Auntie replied kindly. "Witchlings never are allowed to have too much power until they learn to use it wisely. In time you will be able to do bigger things." After reading more of the paper, she announced, "According to the newspaper, the carnival is going to be open tonight. You will have to go back, and ruin it again."

Witcheena's eyes narrowed. She intended to visit the carnival anyway. But if she appeared eager to go, her aunt might be suspicious, and send her somewhere else. After thinking hard for a way to fool the old witch, she said slyly, "Do I have to go there? Shouldn't I haunt some other place?"

Auntie peered over the newspaper at her niece for a long time. But she said, "Well, I will read on. Maybe there is something else you can do." Moments later she exclaimed, "Oh, bats! Another one of those Unidentified Flying Objects was sighted last night. UFOs, my foot! You and I know they are space ships from Mars. How dare those little green men fly into our territory! Haunting the earth and scaring folks is our job. Remind me to tell the ladies when they come for brew tomorrow night. We simply must do something about these foreign tourists!"

"Yes, ma'am." Witcheena closed her eyes so her aunt would not see how they sparkled. What a joke! If only Auntie knew the reported Unidentified Flying Object was her own niece zipping about in a carnival Moon Ship! She covered her mouth to keep from cackling. It was not often she could keep a secret from her all-knowing aunt.

"Did you see this UFO pest last night?" her aunt asked.

Witcheena looked at the ceiling. "No, ma'am. I didn't see a single solitary Unidentified Flying Object anywhere. And that's the truth. And I was in bed by midnight."

"Well, dearie," her aunt continued, "I am sorry, but you will have to return to the carnival. I can't find another thing for you to do tonight."

"Oh, all right," Witcheena answered, pretending she didn't care. She got up and kissed her aunt. "May I go now?"

"Yes, but be back by midnight."

"I promise."

Witcheena put her pointed hat on over the beanie, and skipped across the barn floor. Joy, joy, joy, she would be seeing Nancy again. She only tripped twice. She noticed the cats and bats were all out. That meant it was a warm night. Many people might attend the carnival on a warm night. It would be great fun to ruin it.

Then her footsteps lagged. "I just can't say hello to Nancy, and then zip off and ruin the carnival. What shall I do?"

She was torn between pleasing herself and Nancy, and obeying her aunt. What a problem! Her first big problem, really. She knew having problems to solve was one of the groans of growing up. But this one was making her head ache. It was no use asking Auntie what to do. And she could not confide in Nancy without betraying her witchhood.

As she straddled the broom, she murmured, "I guess I will have to figure things out all alone."

8

CADENZA gave her a smooth ride to the shadowy edge of the carnival grounds. Witcheena set the broom comfortably against a telephone pole. Quickly she changed into an earthling wearing blue denim stretch pants, a red middy blouse, and red-and-white striped tennis shoes.

Nancy was waiting for her near the Ferris wheel. She was wearing light blue pants and a pink-and-blue flowered shirt. The two greeted each other with squeals of joy.

"Did you come on the bus?" Witcheena asked.

"Yes. Did you?"

"No, I flew over on my broom."

Nancy giggled. "Oh, you and your witch talk!" She pointed to the crowds all around them. "Look how many people are here tonight. I bet they all came, hoping to see that Unidentified Flying Object.

Did you see it?" Before Witcheena could answer, she hurried on. "I wonder if it was a real flying saucer. Wouldn't it be simply marvelous if it appeared again tonight? It just must appear, and early enough so I can see it."

Witcheena rolled her eyes, and said brashly, "Cross your fingers, and maybe it will." A tremendously exciting thought raced through her head. She would fly the Moon Ship while Nancy and thousands of others were watching. Immediately she began scheming.

Meantime Nancy shouted over the noise, "Come on! Let's buy some popcorn." She plunged into the crowd.

Witcheena wormed her way slowly past many boys and girls. All the while she was thinking hard. Soon she turned and went in a different direction which brought her to the Moon Ship ride. She stamped her foot, said the magic words for blow-wind-blow, and drew a circle in the air with one finger. Immediately a small dust storm enveloped the carnival grounds. Under cover of the flying dust and sawdust, she darted behind the tent, clambered into the Moon Ship, and snapped the hatch. She quaked so with excitement that she stuttered when she said the magic words. The little space ship shot upward like a rocket. After the dust settled below, she made the module swirl and swoop, and even fly upside down. Then she grew bolder, and zoomed so low that she almost scraped paint off the Ferris wheel.

The people on the carnival grounds pointed excitedly. Boys and girls jumped up and down, and waved wildly. She waved back. But suddenly the blinding light from one of the huge spotlights on the ground below surrounded her. Even with her sunglasses on, she couldn't see. And what if Nancy recognized her and the Moon Ship? Frightened, she flew away from the light. Anyway, she had been gone long enough. Nancy must be wondering where she was.

She shoved the control wheel forward, opened the hatch an inch, and pointed a finger at the ground surrounding the Moon Ship ride. As she stamped her foot and said the magic blow-dust-blow words again, dirt swirled about the tent. In two seconds she landed, hopped out, and disappeared into the crowd. When she reached the booth where popcorn was sold, Nancy shrieked at her, "I saw it! I saw it! Did you see it? Wasn't it the most exciting thing you ever saw?"

Witcheena almost purred with pleasure. Nancy was happy now. All the boys and girls were happy.

Doing something nice with her witch power made her feel warm all over. Maybe she should do something nice more often!

Nancy wished aloud for the flying saucer to come back. "Come back, come back. Pretty please, come back," she crooned.

"It won't come back, and it wasn't a flying saucer. It was a moon ship," Witcheena said.

"How do you know it wasn't a flying saucer?" Nancy demanded.

"By the shape. Flying saucers are saucer-shaped and have a row of flashing red and green lights around the middle."

"Do you suppose it was a moon ship from another planet that got off track some way, and flitted down here?" Nancy's face turned pale. She looked frightened. "Maybe there were Martians aboard. But I still don't care! I want it to come back."

Witcheena remarked a little crossly, "Aren't you ever satisfied? Wasn't seeing it once enough? I am not going to fly that thing once more just for you. It's too dangerous. That bright floodlight almost blinded me. Witches can't stand bright lights shining straight in their eyes."

Then she gulped, and froze. She had babbled too much again.

Nancy's jaw fell open. Her lips trembled. "I . . . I don't know whether to believe you, or not. Sometimes your witch talk scares me. Sometimes I think you're fibbing. But right now I think maybe you're telling the truth! But you couldn't be! You aren't really a witch."

"You don't believe I flew that . . . that thingamajig?" Witcheena croaked. The tone of her voice made her afraid she had already started to turn into a toad.

"No," Nancy said positively. "Let's forget the whole subject. Let's go ride the Ferris wheel."

Once more Witcheena sighed with relief. But her knees shook as she followed Nancy through the crowd. After their ride, the two strolled along the Street of Fun. It was lined with booths where men offered them chances to win prizes. Witcheena spied an enormous purple rabbit. It was sitting on the counter of a booth. "Look at that rabbit. It's almost as big as I am."

"How I'd love to have it!" Nancy exclaimed. "I have two quarters left. I am going to spend both trying to win it." She gave the man fifty cents. In return, she received ten plastic rings. She tossed each one at the target, which was a smaller mechanical rabbit. To win, she must drop one of her rings over the rabbit's enormous ears while it rocked back and forth. She tossed and tossed. Not one ring caught on the ears. She was so disappointed that tears filled her eyes.

Witcheena could not bear to see Nancy in tears. Not when she could make her happy by using certain magic words. Of course, if she got caught, she might turn into a toad. But who would hear her? A quick glance assured her that her aunt was not close by. Besides, she had an uncontrollable urge to show off in front of Nancy. So she put one quarter on the counter and received five rings. "Watch this," she boasted. She stamped her foot, said the magic words, and threw the first ring. It settled over the mechanical rabbit's ears.

Nancy squealed. "You did that just like a witch!"

Immediately there was a terrible racket, like a thousand bones rattling angrily.

Witcheena turned pink-and-green. She knew that awful sound. It was her aunt rattling her bones! Her invisible aunt. Was Auntie ever mad! So her aunt knew she had disobeyed. Worst of all, she had caught her niece appearing as an earthling, and saying magic words out loud. For that she would be punished.

She looked down at her tennis shoes fearfully.

Any moment they would turn into toad's feet.

However, neither the man in the booth nor Nancy had paid any attention to the noise because it was so noisy everywhere around them. The man handed the big purple rabbit to Witcheena. She gave it to Nancy. "Here . . . it's something to remember me by."

"Oh, I can't thank you enough," Nancy cried. "I'm sorry I called you a witch. You're not a witch. But you look awful. Are you sick to your stomach?"

Witcheena swayed. Once more she was saved from turning into a toad. But she still had to face her aunt. "I . . . I think I better go home."

"Me, too. It's nearly curfew time. But let's meet tomorrow."

Witcheena shook her head. "I won't be allowed to come to the carnival again."

Nancy thought a moment. "Then let's meet at the place where the new amusement park is going to be built. My father told me he would take me to see it, maybe tomorrow night."

Witcheena had a hunch her aunt would never let her see Nancy again. "I'll meet you if I can. Where is the new park to be?"

Nancy could not remember exactly. "Look in the newspaper." She waved Witcheena off. "I hope you feel better. And thank you ever so much for winning the rabbit for me. Goodbye."

"Goodbye," Witcheena said forlornly, positive she would never see Nancy again.

Minutes later she reached the telephone pole where she had parked Cadenza. Since it was dark

there, she changed back into her witchling clothes. It was no use putting out the carnival lights now. She climbed on the broom, and said, "Let's go home, Cadenza."

Cadenza bucked her off into the dirt.

Witcheena climbed on again, and grabbed the broom handle as hard as she could. Cadenza gave her the worst ride of her entire life. When she stepped into the barn and called Angela, the cat hissed at her and ran off.

Witcheena burst out crying. Just because she had done something nice for a change, everybody in witchdom hated her! Sobbing, she ran to her room, threw herself on her bed, and cried herself to sleep. Of course, she didn't wet her pillow. She cried dry, as always.

9

THE NEXT evening Witcheena dragged down to the kitchen. There was no fire burning brightly, no stew bubbling fragrantly. Auntie was rocking. Her face was as dark as a thundercloud. Witcheena slunk to her chair, and waited.

Auntie kept rocking, without saying a word.

Witcheena trembled. If only her aunt would scold her. Maybe Auntie was mad enough to turn her into a toad. *Snick!* Just like that. The thought was so horrible that Witcheena wailed, "Oooooh!"

"Stop that howling," Auntie said crossly.

That made Witcheena bawl even louder. "W-why don't y-you turn me into a t-toad, and get it over with?"

Auntie stopped rocking. Her stern look crumpled. "I would never do such a horrible thing. Don't you know I love you dearly? I know, I am an old witch, and I look cranky. But I have not forgotten that I was young once long ago, and made mistakes."

"You still love me? After all the naughty things I did?"

"Yes, I still love you. Fortunately no one heard you say the magic words, thanks to all the noise."

Witcheena bounded onto her aunt's lap and hugged her. "I love you, too, and I am truly sorry I was naughty."

A tender look softened the old witch's face. "But I was hurt to see you changed into an earthling. Aren't you happy being a witch?"

Witcheena twiddled her fingers, and twisted her skirt. Finally she confessed in a whispery voice, "Not always."

"What!" The word sounded like cloth tearing.

The little witchling was frightened. However, she summoned her courage and faced her aunt. "I changed into an earthling because I was lonesome. You go off witching every night without me. You have your friends, but I have only Angela and Cadenza. They can't talk."

Auntie's eyes flashed sparks. "You want to change into an earthling forever?"

Witcheena hung her head. She did, and she didn't.

Auntie reminded her, "If you desert your witch-hood, you will be entirely on your own."

The thought of having to lose Auntie and Angela and Cadenza and her mother hurt terribly. "I couldn't leave you," she protested, clinging to her aunt.

The two rocked for a long time.

After a while, Witcheena said, "Couldn't I have an earth playmate now and then? And wear pretty clothes? Couldn't I be a . . . a friendly witch?"

Her Aunt snorted. "I never heard of such a thing."

Witcheena grew bolder. "You and your friends are always groaning about how times change. Can't witches change, too?"

"Not us older witches. We want to go on as we are forever. What would millions of children do without us witches, and our brooms and cats? Hallowe'en would be no fun at all! No, no, no! We must stay as we are." Then she quirked an eyebrow. "Are you trying to talk me out of punishing you? Well, it won't work."

Witcheena backed off to her own chair. "What are you going to do to me?"

Auntie explained she was not going to do anything. Her young niece must set her own punishment.

Witcheena's chin began to tremble. She knew she

had been very naughty. So the punishment would have to be very severe. "I have to give up my new friend?"

Auntie nodded.

Just then there was the sound of flitting and squeaking outside the apartment door. Auntie squawked, "My friends are here for their Thursday party, and I haven't done a thing to get ready." She jabbed her finger in several directions. A fire blazed, and a big kettle of brew steamed. A table set with goodies appeared, and five fancy chairs. "Let them in. Don't keep them waiting."

"Why don't they come right through the door?"

Auntie whispered, "Because this is a party. You never barge in on a party."

Witcheena opened the door. Five bats swooshed inside, and immediately appeared on the chairs as witches. Since this was a party, all were wearing dangling earrings, clanking bracelets, and flowered stockings. They chattered noisily about the weather, and how nice the table looked, and how delicious the brew smelled. They swapped recipes and pills, and cackled over the things they had done since the last get-together.

All this while Witcheena sat quietly on her chair. When Auntie winked, she served the brew. She also passed the plates of goodies, which were chocolate-covered bees and frosted beetles. When the talk grew noisy again, she served herself and returned to her chair. The bees tasted better than that awful imitation hot dog she had eaten at the carnival. But the thought of earth food reminded her of Nancy, and she felt sad.

She guessed it must be about time for Nancy and her father to be looking over the new amusement park site. A quick glance at the wall clock told her it was 6:45 P.M. Yes, they must be there already. She wondered where the site could be. Unfortunately she had not found out. It would not be polite to read the newspaper while her aunt was entertaining company. So she sat with her pointed shoes together, and her hands folded in her lap, like a little lady. She thought of all the fun with Nancy she was missing.

Her aunt's company cackled louder and louder. Witcheena wished she dared stick her fingers in her ears. But that would not be polite, so she rocked. Being excluded from the witches' talk made her feel lonelier than ever.

Not long after there was a loud knocking on the apartment door. The witches jumped up in alarm. They looked through the wood. "It is a man and a girl!" they squeaked. "What can we do? We're too full of goodies to change into bats. We couldn't fly."

Witcheena peered through the wood, and gasped. "It's my friend Nancy and her father!"

"What are they doing here?" Auntie hissed.

"I don't know. I never told Nancy where I lived. They are supposed to be looking over the site for a

new amusement park." Then her eyes widened with horror. "Oh, no! This can't be the place."

The knocking sounded again.

"What are we to do?" wailed Auntie. "It won't do to make ourselves invisible because we've been making too much noise. But if we let them in and they see us, we will all turn to toads. We're trapped!"

The other witches hissed at Witcheena. "Yes, we are trapped, and it's all your fault!"

10

WITCHEENA tried hard to think of a way to save her aunt and the other witches. Suddenly she snapped her fingers. "Change into earth ladies having a tea party. Hurry!"

"Never!" The witches shuddered at the awful suggestion.

"Please," Witcheena pleaded. "It's the only way." She cleared her throat, and called out in an earthling's voice, "Just a min-ute. I'm coming." Then she changed into an earth girl wearing a blue velvet party dress and white slippers.

Auntie switched next, and signaled the others. Whoooosh! Four appeared as earth ladies with fancy hair styles, flowered dresses, and teacups in their hands. The fifth changed into a Siamese cat. The goodies changed into frosted tea cakes, and the black pot of brew into a shiny copper tea kettle.

Witcheena then opened the door, and pretended to be surprised. "Nancy! Where did you come from?"

The two hugged each other, and laughed. Nancy introduced her father, Mr. Brown.

Witcheena invited them into the apartment. "This is my aunt. She's having a tea party. The ladies were talking so loudly that they were surprised when you knocked."

"Please sit down," Auntie said. She raised a finger to make two chairs appear. Witcheena stopped her just in time. "Take our chairs," she suggested.

Mr. Brown bowed to her aunt. "You have a beautiful niece, Mrs. . . ."

"Missus, my foot! I'm an old maid and proud of it," Auntie interrupted.

Witcheena coughed. "My aunt's name is Smith . . . uh . . . . Clementine Smith."

"Clementine! Awk!" Auntie snorted and made a face.

Witcheena gave her a dark look. Then she explained to Mr. Brown, "She hates the name of Clementine."

"Well, as I was saying, Miss Smith," he continued, "you have a beautiful niece. But no wonder. She has such a beautiful and charming aunt."

Auntie was stunned. She had never heard an earth

person say anything nice about a witch. Her sour look melted. She twitched her beads. "Oh, thank you. I always said my niece was beautiful, but I didn't know people thought she took after me." In a syrupy voice she introduced Mr. Brown to her friends. He bowed to each one, and paid each a compliment. Within minutes all were purring and preening. Witcheena had a hard time keeping her face straight.

Nancy spied the Siamese cat. "You do have a Siamese! Did you just get her?"

Witcheena giggled. "Yes, she's a brand new addition."

Nancy swept up the cat, hugged her, and sat down with her on her lap. The cat hissed, and leaped away.

Knowing witches hate to be touched by earth people, Witcheena apologized. "Please excuse Clara. You know how Siamese cats are. So snooty, until they accept you."

Nancy laughed. "You don't have to tell me about cats." She looked around. "My, you have an attractive apartment. Daddy and I never would have guessed anyone lived here, if we hadn't heard the ladies' voices."

Auntie served Nancy and her father tea and cakes. "I am glad you like our little hideaway. If I do say so, I have some talent for interior decorating."

"And for making tea cakes," Nancy exclaimed, helping herself to a second. "These are out of this world."

"Of course, they're out of this world! I whipped them up on the spur of the moment."

Witcheena smothered another giggle.

Mr. Brown said in a more serious voice, "We apologize for intruding on your lovely party. We had no idea people still lived on this old farm. Didn't there used to be a fine old house up on the hill behind here?"

Auntie nodded, and changed the subject. "Tell me, Mr. Brown. How did you and your daughter happen to come here?"

Mr. Brown explained, "This property has been purchased for a new children's amusement park. I am afraid you will have to move right away. Men are coming tomorrow to tear down the barn, and clear out the wrecked cars. But I can have my crew move your furniture, if that would help," he offered. "Perhaps you could stay in a motel until you find another place."

"Thank you, but a motel would never do. We have twenty-six cats and forty-twelve bats," Auntie informed him.

Nancy whooped. "That's what you told me, and I thought you were joking," she told Witcheena. "Do you really have that many cats?"

Auntie was annoyed. "Did you ever hear of a witch who didn't have cats and bats?"

Witcheena gulped. The ladies set down their cups noisily on their tea plates, and started coughing. Mr. Brown looked very confused. Only Nancy laughed. "Oh, your aunt talks the same kooky way you do," she said to Witcheena.

Everyone relaxed. The moment of danger passed. Mr. Brown rose and said goodbye to the ladies. "I am very sorry you and your niece have to move, Miss Smith. Please call on me if there is any way I can be of help."

Nancy said to Witcheena, "Can you come with us? Maybe we can give Daddy some good ideas for the park."

Witcheena wanted to badly. However, she said, "I belong here with Auntie. I must help her."

Nancy understood. "Let's plan to meet the day the new park opens. I'll look for you by the Ferris wheel. Goodbye."

Immediately after they left, the ladies turned back into witches. Every one, except Auntie, hissed at

Witcheena. "This is all your fault. If you hadn't made friends with that dreadful earthling, we wouldn't have had to change into earth ladies. And your aunt wouldn't have to give up her nice home."

Witcheena's chin began to quiver.

Clara, the one who had turned into a cat, said angrily, "It will be a long time before I vote to promote you to Junior Witch rank."

"That will be enough, Clara," Auntie said sharply. "Witcheena knows what she has done, and is truly sorry. I think she saved the day for all of us by having us change into earth ladies enjoying a party. I'm sure Mr. Brown and his daughter don't suspect a thing. After all, none of you were doing anything helpful, with all your Senior Witch powers. And don't forget. I almost betrayed my witchhood. If Nancy hadn't been used to Witcheena's silly talk, I might have had to turn into a toad! And another thing, Witcheena had absolutely nothing to do with our having to move. So don't be harsh on our little witchling. She is very precious to us." She put her arm around Witcheena.

Clara sniffed. "I hated being touched by that earthling."

"For an earthling, she was rather nice," Auntie

remarked. "Her father, too. I must confess I liked my pretty dress. It's been centuries since I had a new one."

Four of the witches agreed they had enjoyed their flowered dresses, but none liked the tea cakes. They were too sweet for witches' teeth. Only Clara would not stop sulking. When she started to pick at Witcheena again, Auntie told her niece, "Don't pay any attention to her. She's just a cranky old witch."

Fortunately it was time for the witches to leave on their scare routes. They said goodbye and flew off. Witcheena dashed into her aunt's arms. "Oh, Auntie, I am sorry I made so much trouble."

"Tush, tush," Auntie soothed her. "We will not talk about it any more. I blame myself for what happened. I should not have sent you alone to ruin that carnival. That was a task for a Senior Witch. I was pushing you into something for which you are not quite ready. From now on, I will let you go your own witchling's pace."

Witcheena felt a little better. But there was something she had to confess. She told her aunt about taking the Moon Ship ride on her own, and being mistaken for an Unidentified Flying Object, and then doing it again for Nancy's sake.

Auntie could not believe it. "How did you make

the Moon Ship fly? You don't know the magic words."

"I made them up." She told Auntie what they were.

Auntie was flabbergasted. "I had no idea you could figure out magic phrases without help. Why, you are a genius!" She sprang out of her rocker,

and hopped about gleefully. "So you were the UFO people saw! Oh, my pet cat! What a joke!" She cackled until she ran out of breath. "Pulling a prank like that on thousands of people will count for a great deal when you are considered for your junior fly-up. But we can't talk any more. We must clean up the party mess and start looking for our new home."

Both flicked their fingers. The tea table, extra chairs, and copper kettle vanished. When the apartment was tidy, they left. Outside Witcheena called Angela. The cat came quickly, and joined the witchling on her broom.

"Ready?" Auntie called from her broom. "Here we go!"

The two took off into the night.

11

Auntie and Witcheena flew, and flew, and flew. They could not find a single place they liked. Just before daylight they returned to the junkyard. "Well, I guess we will have to forget about an apartment for the time being, and hide in the trees during the daytime. Thank goodness, it is spring and the leaves are out."

Witcheena groaned. Tree perching was uncomfortable and noisy. There was no protection from the rain, either.

Auntie grumped. "'You'd think there would be some empty attic, or even a cave somewhere in this county which we could fix up."

Witcheena's eyes widened. "There is a cave! I forgot all about it. It's right over in those rocks, among the trees. Angela found it one night when we were playing hide and seek."

The two leaned their brooms against the rocks and followed the cat through the crack into the cave. Auntie started a fire burning immediately. After she looked around, she said, "It is rather small but I can manage that." She rotated a bony finger like a dentist drill, said the magic words, and cleaned out two cavities in the far wall. "There! Now we can use the cave for our combination kitchen and living room, and turn those two alcoves into bedrooms."

The dust clouds raised by the drilling made Witcheena sneeze so hard her two hats fell off. "How will the bats get in and out?"

"That's no problem. I'll make a hole in the roof. It will draw off the dust." The moment Auntie drilled the hole in the roof of the cave, the dust swirled out. Then the bats swarmed in because it was almost daylight outside.

As much as she liked bats, Witcheena didn't want any swooping down to cling to her hair. Auntie promptly conjured up an overhead canopy of cobwebs. "Cobwebs are awfully oldfashioned, Auntie. Couldn't we have something modern? What do you think of this?" She conjured up a bright red-gold-and-white striped awning like the one covering the merry-go-round at the carnival. There was plenty of room between it and the roof of the cave for the bats.

"It's beautiful," Auntie exclaimed. "We still don't have a place for the cats to perch. Let's see . . ."

"Let me thing of something," Witcheena pleaded. She thought and thought. Suddenly she clapped her hands. She conjured up a small Ferris wheel which fitted into the opposite corner of the cave. In place of seats, she included baskets lined with catnip-scented pillows. "Do you like it?" she asked Angela.

Angela leaped onto the wheel and settled herself in a basket. "Meow-rrrr," she mewed, meaning she liked it very much.

Witcheena called, "Here, kitties. Come see your new home."

One by one they slipped down the hole in the roof onto the canopy. They walked around on the canopy, yowling, until Witcheena fixed an opening for them just above the Ferris wheel. Each squeezed through that, slithered over the wheel and settled in a basket. They purred loudly to show how much they liked their new home. As their yellow and green eyes glowed in the firelight, the Ferris wheel twinkled just like the one on the carnival grounds.

Auntie was astonished. "How artistic you are, dearie! Just wait until my friends see this. But quickly now. Stamp your feet and say the magic words with me. We must move our furniture and belongings over here at once."

Moments later the beds, cabinet and rockers appeared. Witcheena tidied her quilt and hung her clothes and two caps on the four posters. By the time Auntie re-arranged the furniture a half-dozen times, she was worn out.

"Auntie, let's quit. You looked tired. You're as white as a ghost."

Her aunt answered peevishly, "A fine thing to say to your old aunt. You know I hate ghosts. But it is time we went to bed."

Unfortunately the two did not get too much sleep. The daytime noise was terrible as work began on the children's amusement park. Bulldozers snarled, men shouted, hammers pounded, and trucks made the ground shake.

That evening after Witcheena finished practicing, she asked, "What may I do tonight?"

"The newspaper says the carnival has moved on into another county," Auntie informed her. "You stick close to home so you won't get into any more trouble. If you practice your broom landings and take-offs, and hiding, the time will pass quickly."

Witcheena pouted. "That's baby stuff." After she

peered through the rocks, she added, "The cars and barn are all gone."

Auntie peered, too. "Well, you just flit out there and put the old barn back together again. And if that's too hard, hide the workmen's tools."

Witcheena burst into tears. "I don't want to play all alone. If I hide the tools, the park will never get finished, and I'll never have any playmates."

Auntie's rocker creaked loudly as she pondered what to do. As a witch, her first thought was to make trouble for the builders. However, many more earthlings would visit the park after it was finished. Then haunting the park would be more important because of the crowds which could be scared.

"Hmmm . . . You did a lot of mischief at the carnival, didn't you?"

Witcheena nodded. "And I could do lots more at an amusement park. I could even scare the children." She told Auntie what Nancy had said about the overnight campground. "She said the boys and girls sit around a fire telling ghost and witch stories. Then they sleep outside in bags. I could hide in the trees and make scary sounds. I . . . I could scare Nancy when she camps overnight with her Girl Scout troop."

"Oh, ho! I see through you. You want the park

finished quickly so you can see your friend again."

That was the reason, Witcheena confessed. Then she added in a small voice, "Is having a playmate so awful?"

"N-no," her aunt decided. "But if you keep on having earthlings for friends, you might want to change into one forever. Then I would lose you. That would break my heart."

Witcheena hopped into her aunt's lap and gave her a big hug. "I would never do that. Honestly! I know now I don't ever want to be an earthling. Poor things! They can't fly, or do all the things we can. They have to eat make-believe hot dogs."

After thinking some more, Auntie gave in. "All right. You pull pranks every night until the park is opened. Afterwards you scare the children who visit it. If you do a good job, I will turn over haunting the park entirely to you. That way you will have lots of playmates for the next hundred years, and can still carry on your witchley duties."

"Can one of the playmates be Nancy?" Witcheena asked quickly while her aunt was in such a good mood.

"We-l-l," Auntie said, "I guess you have learned your lesson. All right. If Nancy comes to the park, you may change into an earthling and play with her."

"Oh, thank you, thank you!" Witcheena kissed her aunt. Then she hopped off her lap and raced through the crack in the rocks, calling, "Angela! Cadenza! We have work to do!"

12

IN THE following weeks bulldozers cleared the areas for the picnic grounds, the volleyball and tennis courts, the baseball diamond, and the carnival rides. The creek gurgled sweetly once more. Workers swarmed everywhere. They built slides and swings, teeter-totters, and jungle gyms, and poured concrete for a large swimming pool. They erected a pavilion for rainy day play and planted acres of grass and flowers.

Witcheena and Angela and Cadenza had great fun flitting about. The little witchling hid tools, and turned sections of the safety fence upside down, and flummoxed the machinery. However, since she wanted the park finished quickly, she was not destructive.

Actually, when the workmen began putting together the steel framework for the Ferris wheel and

merry-go-round and Moon Ship ride, she helped
by putting the seats and ponies and modules in
place. Then when the Moon Ship ride was finished,
she hopped about it like a happy grasshopper.

"Guess what," she said to Angela, "I am going to
take you for a ride in a Moon Ship."

Angela hissed.

"Oh, once you get used to it, you'll love it. It's the
modern way to fly."

The cat arched her back and stuck her tail straight
up.

"But I must practice flying a Moon Ship," Witcheena told her. "How can I ever become a Pioneer witch like my mother if I don't? The astronauts practiced months before they flew to the moon. I should, too. I know there aren't any children on the moon yet, but there're bound to be some later on. They'll need witches up there, so I want to be ready. If I volunteer for a real moon flight, I would need you and Cadenza for company. A witch isn't a witch without her cat and broom. So please fly with me now."

Angela stopped hissing and twitched her tail. That meant she was thinking.

"If you went to the Moon or to Mars or Venus, you'd be the most famous cat in the whole world," Witcheena reminded her.

Angela liked the idea of becoming the most famous cat in the world. She leaped up on the little gumdrop-shaped Moon Ship and meowed at Witcheena impatiently. Moments later Angela and Cadenza and Witcheena were settled on the couches with the seat belts fastened. When the ship lifted off the ground, Angela dug her claws into the upholstery. But she soon relaxed and enjoyed looking out the window.

Witcheena guided the craft up above the smog

so they all could see the stars more clearly. "Isn't it cozy in here?" Cadenza swayed a little. Because it was dry and warm in the module, she didn't have to strain to keep from warping. Angela purred because her silken coat was not getting wet and matted. After a long ride, Witcheena returned the Moon Ship to its proper place. But she had a terrible time making Angela leave. The cat had a regular tantrum. She liked the modern way of flying. Witcheena coaxed and coaxed, and finally said, "If you don't ride on Cadenza any more, her feelings will be hurt. Come on, now. Be a good cat. I will take both of you on lots more flights."

"Meow?" Angela asked.

"I promise," Witcheena said, crossing her fingers. Then, to be sure Cadenza's feelings weren't hurt, they took a ride on the broom. At midnight Witcheena put Cadenza by the crack in the rock, and she and Angela went to bed. It hurt the broom to bend in order to squeeze through the jagged entry into the cave, so that is why Witcheena left her outside. But the next evening when she and Angela slipped outside again, the broom was missing. "Ca-den-za," she called worriedly. "Where are you?"

There was a rattling sound nearby. Witcheena found the broom on a pile of scrap lumber in the middle of a large pit. She picked her up and petted her. "Whatever happened? Did the workmen toss you on this scrap pile?"

Cadenza's splinters bristled. She jerked once. That meant "Yes."

As Witcheena looked about, she discovered the area in front of the big rock had changed greatly. Now there was a tall metal lamp post near the entrance to the cave. That was too bad, because it would be hard to come and go without being seen if the light was turned on after dark. About twenty steps from it was the large pit. On the far side of it were six small log cabins. On each, three walls were lined with bunks. The fourth wall was missing, so those lying on the bunks could see out.

While Witcheena and Angela flitted in and out of the cabins, they heard voices. That was strange. No one ever came near the park after dark. Then one by one, lights flashed on all over. The one beside the cave flooded the rock and pit and cabins. Witcheena was blinded for a moment. Angela snarled, and bounded off.

As the voices grew louder, Witcheena recognized one. It was Nancy's! Quickly the little witchling scuttled behind one cabin. She placed Cadenza against a wall, and waited for her friend to appear. When she saw what Nancy was wearing, she pictured herself in the same outfit. Seconds later she changed into an earthling wearing faded blue jeans cut off above the knees, a sloppy shirt, and thonged sandals. "Bats!" Her long stockings showed until she used her power to make them disappear.

Nancy was with her father and a small group of men. They examined the light pole and cabins. Witcheena swished off, and then appeared on the path. She did not want them to think she had been prowling around the unlighted park alone.

"Yoo-hoo, Nancy," she called out.

Everyone turned. Nancy squealed, and ran toward her. The two hugged each other.

"I was riding by on my bicycle and saw the lights, so I came in to see what was going on," Witcheena fibbed.

"Daddy and members of the Inspection Committee had to check the new light poles, so I came with them," Nancy explained.

Witcheena said hello to Mr. Brown and the others.

"What do you think of the park Daddy built? Isn't it scrumptious? It opens in only two days. I can hardly wait. Don't you adore this overnight camping spot?"

"Is that what it is?" Witcheena asked.

"Yes. This is where I will camp overnight with my Girl Scout Troop. Remember, I told you about it. We will spread our sleeping bags on the bunks in the cabins. We will cook our hot dogs over the campfire in the pit. After dark we will sit around the fire and tell ghost and witch stories." She looked at the dark trees towering over the campsite. "If only we had a Resident Witch to scare us, everything would be perfect."

"A Resident Witch? What kind of witch is that?"

Nancy thought a moment. "That's a witch who lives in one place forever, and if we had one here, she would have to scare the campers every night."

"Really?" Witcheena's heart began to beat rapidly. She had never heard of such a thing. A Resident Witch? What a marvelous idea! The thought made her heart beat even faster. She must find out more. "Where would the Resident Witch live in the daytime? There is no Witch House here. If your witch had to be up late scaring campers, she would need some place to sleep during the day."

Nancy giggled. "Oh, I was just fooling. A Resident Witch is something I made up."

"But having a Resident Witch in the park is a super-dooper idea."

Nancy nodded slowly. "You are right!" She interrupted a conversation her father was having with the committee. "Daddy, listen. I just thought of something. Why not build a witch house, and advertise there will be a genuine witch here every night to scare campers?" She danced up and down. "Isn't that a marvelous idea?"

Mr. Brown smiled. One of the committee men said, "We could put a sign on one of the cabins saying *Witch House—Keep Out*."

"I'm afraid that wouldn't do," Witcheena said politely. "A witch would never live in a house that near people. Children know that. A witch house has to be tucked away somewhere, out of reach. A witch can't have children running in and out all day while she is sleeping."

Mr. Brown rubbed his chin. "We're awfully rushed right now, Nancy. But we might build a witch house somewhere on the grounds later on."

Nancy stamped her foot. "But I want it built right away so it will be where I can see it when I come to camp overnight."

"We'll see," her father said patiently.

"And I have another wonderful idea! On opening night, let's have a contest in the open-air theater. Let's have boys and girls and old ladies put on witch acts. The one who has the best act could be crowned Resident Witch, and receive a year's free tickets to the carnival rides."

The committee thought that might stir up a lot of interest in the park. Mr. Brown said, "We like your idea, Nancy. We will have the contest on opening night, and build the witch house as soon after as we can. The Mayor promised that all rides would be free on opening night, so there is sure to be a crowd. Having the contest would be a nice way to finish off the fun."

Nancy hugged Witcheena. "Can you meet me here opening night? By the Ferris wheel?"

Witcheena promised.

The committee had nothing more to inspect so everyone headed for the gate. Mr. Brown asked Witcheena, "Could we drive you home?"

"No, thank you. I . . . I came on my bicycle," she fibbed.

Nancy exclaimed, "I'm so glad we're going to see each other again. Goodbye for now."

"Goodbye," Witcheena sang out. She waved as every one drove away.

Instantly she changed back to her witchling clothes. Since she had to pick up Cadenza at the campsite, she skipped back to the broom. She only tripped once. Angela answered her call. Then the two flew off on Cadenza to locate Auntie and tell her the good news.

13

WITCHEENA found Auntie disturbing the air waves around the television towers. This made the stations' pictures wobble. They flew to a tree in a cemetery to talk.

The old witch was delighted to hear about the witch house. But she was even more interested in Nancy's idea of a Resident Witch. "That earthling has some very good ideas. In all the hundreds of years I have been a witch, I never heard of a Resident Witch. It is a perfect career for you, dearie."

"For me!" Witcheena gasped. "But I'm not a full-fledged witch. I'm not even a Junior Witch yet."

"I know, but I have more work than I can handle. Adding the amusement park to my scare route and having to be there every night would be a real burden. Still, haunting the park is a must. You be the

Resident Witch. That will keep you busy and close to home where a witchling should be. If you do a good job, I will discuss the position with my friends. If they approve, we might introduce a bill at the convention to have it given a permanent rank in witchdom. Then if the idea is accepted, you will have the place of honor as the first official Resident Witch in our world."

Witcheena was stunned. Her mouth hung open so long that a moth flew in and out. She threw her arms about her aunt's neck. "I promise to do my very best. I will think hard about different ways to haunt the park. I will use my imagination."

After a moment, she added, "I know what my first task will be. On the night the park opens, there is going to be a contest to choose an earthling as the Resident Witch. Any boy or girl or old lady may enter the contest. What if a boy should win? Or some jolly fat lady?"

Auntie rattled her bones. "That would be terrible! Maybe you better make it rain so the contest would have to be cancelled."

Witcheena puckered her lips. "Making it rain is oldfashioned. I'll think of something. A witch simply has to win that contest."

"Well, you think hard while I get back to my scare

route. Toodle-eee-ooo, dearie," Auntie said, and flew off on her broom.

Witcheena and Angela flew home on Cadenza. Angela wanted to play tag around the merry-go-round. "No, I have to use my imagination," Witcheena told her. So the two sat on the opposite ends of the teeter-totter, and made it teeter-and totter slowly. This was so relaxing that very soon Witcheena sprouted a new idea. "I have decided to built the witch house myself," she announced. "The carpenters are sure to build a log cabin, just like the ones at the campground. Who ever heard of a log cabin witch house? Ridiculous!"

The two flitted on Cadenza to the top of the rocks. After thinking very hard some more, Witcheena said, "I know exactly what I want." She stamped her foot, said the magic words, and pointed. Immediately there was a loud racket as the house took shape over the bats' and cats' entrance to the cave. The steep A-shaped roof was covered with shingles. The small windows were curtained with cobwebs. The front door swung on a hinge so the cats and bats could come and go easily. The color of the outside walls blended nicely with the rocks and the overhanging pine branches.

"Does it look witch-like enough?" she asked Angela.

The cat blinked her eyes. "Meow-rrrr."

Next Witcheena rode Cadenza down to the overnight camping site. She skipped around, making sure the campers could see the house when they were nestled in their sleeping bags, or sitting around the fire. Then she called the cat to her side. "Will you stay down here while I go back up to the Witch House and make witch noises? Tell me if you think the boys and girls can hear me clearly."

Witcheena practiced her shrieks and moans and cackles. Angela flickered her eyes to let the little witchling know when she sounded too weak, or too loud. After a while Witcheena exclaimed, "Whew! I'm tired. Let's rest." She sat down with her pointed shoes dangling over the edge. Angela scampered up the steep rocks, and snuggled down in her lap.

Moments later Witcheena said, "I have a wonderful idea! Come on." The two hopped on Cadenza and flew to the wide gate at the entrance of the park. There Witcheena told Angela, "I am going to do something just for you." She went through her magic routine. Immediately a large white sign appeared on the gate. Bold black letters read NO DOGS

ALLOWED. Witcheena cackled. "There! What do you think of that?"

Angela leaped onto her shoulder and licked her ear.

After that they all returned to the Witch House. Witcheena sighed happily, "I can hardly wait to start scaring the campers. My, I hope they like me."

Then a dark thought made her frown. What if the children didn't like her? If they didn't, they wouldn't pay any attention when she cackled and shrieked and scared them. Then she would fail as a Resident Witch. This worried her greatly. She must be successful, or the new rank would never be accepted at the national convention. Once more she thought hard. Then certain ideas began to blossom in her head. Her eyes glowed with mischievous excitement. At long last she knew exactly what she was going to do!

Angela meowed.

Witcheena cackled. "No, I am not going to tell you one single thing. For once I am going to keep a secret all to myself."

14

THE EVENING the new park opened, hundreds of boys and girls, parents and grandparents, aunts and uncles and cousins poured through the gate. Witcheena watched from inside the Witch House until she spied Nancy. Quickly she pictured herself in an outfit like her friend's—white shorts with no long stockings showing, white sleeveless blouse, and white sandals. She slid down the tree-shadowed side of the steep rocks, passed the secret place where Cadenza was hidden out of the reach of prying boys, and changed into a girl earthling. She ran her hands over her face, arms and legs so they turned sun-tan color. Then she wormed her way through the crowd to the Ferris wheel.

"Yoo, hoo, Nancy," she called.

For the next hour the two tried everything in the park except the swimming pool. They swung and teeter-tottered, clambered through the jungle gyms, slid down slides, and sampled all the rides in the carnival section. Nancy exclaimed over the Witch House. "I didn't know Daddy had it built. Isn't it witch-like looking?"

Suddenly a voice boomed out from a loud speaker. "Boys and girls and grown-ups, it is time for the Witch Contest. Please come to the outdoor theater at once."

The theater had a medium-sized stage and water-proofed curtain. Out in front were many rows of benches. These were so jammed with children that Witcheena and Nancy had to stand at the back. Mr. Brown stepped out from behind the curtain. He welcomed every one to the park. He explained about the contest for Resident Witch. Then he asked, "Will you like having a Resident Witch haunt the over-night camp site?"

"Yes!" the children shouted, clapped and whistled.

Mr. Brown held up his hands so everyone quieted. "Each contestant has three minutes to do his or her act. You will judge each one on appearance, voice, and acting ability. Clap for the one you like best. Ready? Here is contestant number one. Her name is Mrs. Flora Jackson." Mr. Brown left the stage.

Before the curtains parted, Witcheena whispered to Nancy, "Are you going to enter the contest?"

"Oh, no. I can't act for sour apples. Are you going to?"

Witcheena rolled her eyes. "Mmmmm—maybe. You'll see."

Mrs. Jackson stepped out from behind the curtain. She wore a white hat, flowered dress and white oxfords. She was fat and jolly. All she did was talk about how much she loved children, and would try to be a good witch. When she bowed and left the stage, two children clapped.

Nancy giggled. "I bet those were her grandchildren."

The next ones were only fair. Some were children wearing capes or blankets wrapped around their shoulders. One wore a witch's costume but galloped about cowboy-fashion on a broom. All tried to cackle. Witcheena held her nose because they were so awful.

Then a Mrs. Graham was announced. Her costume was so good that for a moment Witcheena thought she might be Auntie in disguise. But after peering harder, she could see it was not her aunt.

Mrs. Graham put a kettle on the stage floor, and removed the lid. Immediately white clouds rose from it.

"How did she do that?" Witcheena said, gasping. She was alarmed. Were earthlings learning witch tricks?

Nancy explained, "She probably used dry ice, or that stuff they use on television to make clouds and fog."

Witcheena relaxed.

Mrs. Graham danced around her kettle. She cackled and shrieked. She sounded so scary that even Witcheena felt cold prickles up and down her back. Some of the younger children began to cry. Nancy whispered, "I bet she wins."

Witcheena decided it was time to carry out her plan. She told Nancy, "Excuse me for a moment. I want to get a drink of water. I'll be right back." As she hurried to the rear of the stage, she could hear the audience applauding loudly for Mrs. Graham. "Oh, dear," she worried.

Moments later she found Mr. Brown. She asked him if she might be a contestant.

He answered, "Yes. There are several ahead of you. You may perform last. That will give you plenty of time to put on your costume. How shall I introduce you?"

Witcheena pressed the tip of her nose. "Hmmmm . . . . as Jane Smith, I guess," then she giggled, "the witchiest witch in the West!"

She hurried over to the carnival section of the park. It was deserted because everyone was attending the contest. She slipped around to the back of the Moon Ship ride, where the extra models were resting on their wooden crates. The moment she hopped into one and snapped the hatch, she began to shiver. What she planned to do was so preposterous that she almost shook her bones out of place. The whole ship shook with her.

"Stop shaking!" she scolded herself. She must carry out her bold scheme. If she didn't, the children would never know what a real witchling looked like. They would never hear a real witch cackle and shriek. They would never know anything but a pretend witch, or an imitation witch. It was time they saw a *real* witch!

But this was extremely dangerous for her to try. Never before in witchdom had a witch purposely appeared *as a witch* before earthlings. If the children believed she really was a witch, then she would turn into a toad, right then and there on the stage. But if they only *accepted* her as the best one to be the Resident Witch, without believing she really was a witch, then she would win the contest!

Summoning every ounce of courage, Witcheena gripped the wheel inside the space ship. First she changed back to being a witchling. Her pointed hat was too big and pressed down on her ears until she bent the peak over. Then she stirred up a little dust and flew to the back of the stage. She touched down so quietly behind Mr. Brown that he did not hear her. He was watching a boy performing on the stage.

"Hi!" Witcheena whispered, after opening the hatch.

Mr. Brown looked over his shoulder, and turned pale.

"Don't be afraid. It's me, Witcheena. I mean, Jane Smith."

Mr. Brown mopped his face with his handkerchief. "For a moment I thought you were a visitor from outer space. Your costume is very convincing." A light patter of applause told him the boy had finished his act. "I will introduce you now. Good luck!"

While Mr. Brown stepped out in front of the curtain to introduce her, Witcheena closed the hatch and moved to the center of the stage. She made the lights dim slowly until it was completely dark. When she heard the curtain part, she stamped and whispered magic words and pointed in several places at once. A high soft whistling sound floated down from overhead. An artificial moon slowly climbed into a starlit sky. Its white light shone down on the silver-colored Moon Ship. Quickly Witcheena made clouds of steam pour from its base and red and green lights flickered. The little craft vibrated as if it was struggling hard to lift off. All over the theater children gasped as it lifted an inch, two inches, six inches . . . But sticking out from it were Witcheena's skinny legs and long striped stockings and pointed shoes with the shiny buckles.

A Moon Ship with feet was so ridiculous that the children shouted with glee.

The shoes clumped across the stage, and tripped. The Moon Ship tipped over. From inside came a loud squawk.

The audience nearly exploded with laughter. But Witcheena didn't. She had squawked because she had bumped her nose.

"N-now for the d-dangerous part," she told herself. She righted the space craft and opened the hatch. The peak of her hat popped out first. The next thing the audience saw was an enormous pair of sunglasses with wide white frames. Behind them was a funny dark face. A very witch-like face, but still a young and funny face. The witch grinned, and showed her teeth. They were covered with sparkling braces.

The children clapped even harder than before.

When Witcheena tried to hop out, her big shoes became entangled. She fell in a heap that exposed her polka-dotted underwear. Her peaked hat fell off, revealing her beanie cap with the propeller on top.

She got up clumsily, gave her brown skirt a twitch and waved at the audience. "Hi, kids. My name is Witcheena. I am your friendly Junior Witch. I am a modern witch. I do not ride an oldfashioned broom. I fly around in a Moon Ship. I do not frighten children until they cry. I scare them until they get all goosepimpley with pleasure. Listen!" She cackled and moaned and shrieked. She made genuine witchling sounds.

The children shivered joyfully and clung to each other. Their eyes were sparkling and none were afraid. They loved Witcheena, and told her so by clapping and shouting wildly. One after another hollered, "We want you for our Resident Witch."

Witcheena took a deep bow. Then she asked, "Do you think I am really and truly a witch?" She held her breath. Their answer could make her turn into a toad. Or, it could bring her centuries of happiness.

The children whistled and stomped and shouted gleefully, "No, no, no!"

Mr. Brown walked onto the stage. He declared her the winner of the Resident Witch contest. After Witcheena took many more bows, he said, "It is almost curfew time, children. Good night. Come again soon."

Witcheena curtsied to Mr. Brown. She blew kisses

to the children. Then she hopped back onto the
Moon Ship, folded over the peak of her hat so she
could slip through the hatch, made the ship rise so
her legs and shoes showed again, and ran off the
stage. The moment she came to a dark place, she
zipped the Moon Ship back to its resting place, and
emerged as an earthling.

When she joined Nancy again, her friend gave
her a big hug. "You fooled me. I thought you really
were a witch. Your costume was marvelous. Did
your aunt make it?"

"No," Witcheena boasted. "I did the whole thing
myself."

"I never heard such cackles and shrieks. You must
have practiced for hours."

"I sure did, for hours and hours," she answered
grinning.

Nancy sighed. "I'm sorry, but I have to go now.
When can we meet again?"

Witcheena told Nancy to let her know when she
would be camping overnight in the park with her
Girl Scout troop. "I will scare the girls for you."

"That would be wonderful. Overnight camping
will be great fun as long as you are the Resident
Witch. Goodbye."

After all the children left and the lights were

turned out, Witcheena and Angela played in the park. They tried everything except the Moon Ship ride. Witcheena had had enough of it for one night.

At midnight she and Angela went to bed.

15

THE NEXT evening Auntie asked, "Who won the Resident Witch contest?"

"I did," Witcheena said proudly. She told the old witch about her daring venture.

Auntie nearly fainted. "You appeared as a real witchling before all those earthlings? I have never heard of anything so bold. It was preposterous!"

"I had to do it," Witcheena answered. "You said I could be the Resident Witch. But I wanted the children to *want* me to be their Resident Witch."

Auntie shivered so that her bones rattled. "That was very very dangerous. I declare, I don't know whether you are a harum-scarum witchling, or a very brave one."

Her niece looked very smug. "All I did was use my imagination."

Auntie rocked for a long time. Then she said

slowly, "I think the time has come for you and me to have a heart-to-heart talk. The ladies are coming tonight for brew. When you tell them what a bold thing you did, do not say anything about your wanting the earthlings to like you. Witches take great pride in being witches. They work very hard to scare animals and children and grown-ups. Earth children are not supposed to like witches. They are supposed to be afraid of them, even though no witch has ever harmed a child."

Witcheena nodded. She knew all this.

Auntie stopped rocking, and whispered, "But do you know something? It's a deep dark secret. I really shouldn't tell you this until you graduate to Senior Witch rank. But really and truly, witches want children to love them."

"Honestly?" Witcheena exclaimed. She had never suspected that. "I thought witches were supposed to have hearts as hard as stone."

"Yes," Auntie assured her. "Really and truly, deep down in their hearts, witches want children's eyes to sparkle when they think of witches. They want them to like witch stories, and being haunted by them. They even like having them pretend to be witches on Hallowe'en."

"For ev-er-more," Witcheena gasped.

"Since you are a witchling, you did not realize how extra-special brave you were in showing yourself as a witch to the children. You were brave to risk turning into a toad. But it was even more brave to show the children that you loved them, and wanted them to love you. That was very special."

Witcheena hopped onto Auntie's lap. The two rocked until they heard the witches landing in the tree above the witch house. Auntie said, "Quick! Go to the door and invite them in. That will give me time to stir up some resfreshments."

Witcheena nipped up through the catway into the Witch House, and opened the door for the guests. "Good evening! Please come in. Auntie is expecting you."

"My, what a charming Witch House," they all exclaimed.

"Thank you. Auntie and I built it."

The moment the witches saw the cats swinging in their baskets on the little Ferris wheel, and the gay striped canopy overhead that kept the bats out of their hair, they cried, "Marvelous!"

Auntie seated them, and after the refreshments were eaten, she said, "Ladies, we have very important business to discuss this evening. Shall we call the meeting to order?"

The hostess always served as president for the business meeting. Auntie conjured up a gavel, and rapped it three times on the table. "Will the meeting please come to order?" After the roll call and the secretary's report, she asked, "It there any new business to come before the meeting?"

"Yes, Madam President," Witcheena spoke up.

Clara scolded, "Be quiet. Witchlings are to be seen and not heard."

President Auntie said, "I grant the witchling permission to speak. She has something important to tell us."

"Let the witchling speak," the others commanded.

Witcheena felt very proud to take part in a meeting of Senior Witches. She stood straight, and didn't fiddle with her skirt. Briefly she explained Nancy's idea of a Resident Witch for the park. Then she asked the witches to please establish a new rank in witchdom, that of Resident Witch. "Think how many children all over the country can be scared if we have Resident Witches at schools and amusement parks."

The witches put their hats together. They talked and talked. They liked the idea, but did not feel it was practical. "We Senior Witches have more work than we can handle already. None of us is getting any younger. We simply cannot devote all our time to being Resident Witches. It's too confining, too limiting. We are afraid it would not work out at all," they decided.

Witcheena was not discouraged. She gave her imagination a good shake, and pulled out another new idea. "Would you allow Junior Witches to serve as Resident Witches? That would give them something to do on their own. This is very important for growing witchlings. It helps them become better witches."

After more talk the witches decided to allow Witcheena to serve a trial period as Resident Witch. If she did a good job, they would present the idea at the national convention.

But Witcheena still was not satisfied. She had a very clever idea. "Wouldn't I have to fly up to Junior Witch rank before I could serve as a Resident Witch?"

All agreed except Clara. She thought Witcheena was still too young and flighty to fly up to the next rank. "I vote no."

Witcheena was crushed.

Auntie came to her rescue. "Tell them how you won the contest, dearie."

When Witcheena did, all the witches except

Auntie rocked so hard that they fell over backwards. After they sat down again, one of them exclaimed, "What a brave thing to do! But what made you do it?"

"I did it for the honor of all witches," she told them. "I could not bear to have the children accept a jolly fat lady or a boy for a Resident Witch. I thought it was time they heard a genuine witch cackle and screech."

President Auntie cleared her throat. "Now shall we vote to admit our witchling to the rank of Junior Witch?"

All voted yes. Even cranky Clara.

Witcheena jumped up. "Am I now a Junior Witch?"

"Not quite." Auntie pulled a box wrapped in fancy paper from under her bed. She handed it to her niece. Inside was a dark green shirt and skirt, and a pointed hat.

"My Junior Witch uniform!" Witcheena hugged and kissed everyone. "May I put it on now?"

"Oh, no. You must wait until the convention. That is when the fly-up ceremony will be held. You will get to meet Junior Witches from all over the country there. You will say the Junior Witch oath with them. You will receive your Junior Witch badge of rank, and learn more secrets of witchdom. Afterwards there will be a party."

"Oh, thank you, everybody," Witcheena said. "I will work very hard to be a good Junior Witch."

After that Auntie said, "It is late. The meeting is adjourned."

When she banged the gavel on the table, the witches swooshed out of the cave. Before Auntie took off on her broom, she said, "One word of advice, dearie. Have a good time. Fly that new-fangled Moon Ship, if you wish. But fly high so you cannot be seen from the city. We don't want children complaining that witches have given up their brooms. Toodle-eeee-oooo!" With a shrill cackle, Auntie took off on her evening scare route.

Moments later Witcheena appeared outside the Witch House. Angela and Cadenza were there. Witcheena spread her arms wide, as if she were hugging the entire park. She had her own world at last—a world of fun and laughter, of lights and music and love. As Resident Witch of the children's amusement park, she would live happily for years to come.